W9-AEE-530

# The Garden That We Grew

by JOAN HOLUB

illustrations by HIROE NAKATA

Viking

This is the garden
that we will grow.

This is the patch
we will plant row by row.

This is the dirt,
all warm and brown.

These are the seeds
we push way down.

This is the water
we spray on the seeds.

These are our hands
that pull out the weeds.

These are the buds
that peek from their beds.

These are the flowers
that poke out their heads.

These are the pumpkins
that grow on the vine.

These are the summer days
filled with sunshine.

These are the worms
that go here and there.

These are the bees
that buzz in the air.

This is the day
we have all waited for.

We pick our pumpkins—
one, two, three, four!

Inside the pumpkins

is wet, orange goop.

This is the way

we scoop, scoop, scoop, scoop!

This is the pie

we make and we munch.

These are the cookies
we bake by the bunch.

These are the faces
that grin ear to ear.

Let's save the seeds . . .

to grow pumpkins next year!

For Julie Hannah and her green thumb—*J.H.*
To my mother M.N.—*H.N.*

VIKING
Published by the Penguin Group
Penguin Putnam Books for Young Readers, 345 Hudson Street,
New York, New York 10014, U.S.A.

Penguin Books Ltd, Registered Offices: Harmondsworth, Middlesex, England

First published in the United States of America by Viking and Puffin Books,
divisions of Penguin Putnam Books for Young Readers, 2001

1  3  5  7  9  10  8  6  4  2

LIBRARY OF CONGRESS CATALOGING-IN-PUBLICATION DATA
Holub, Joan.
The garden that we grew / by Joan Holub ; pictures by Hiroe Nakata.
p.  cm.
Summary: Children plant pumpkin seeds, water and weed the garden patch,
watch the pumpkins grow, pick them, and enjoy them in various ways.
ISBN 0-670-89799-X (hardcover)
[1. Pumpkin—Fiction. 2. Gardening—Fiction. 3. Stories in rhyme.]
I. Nakata, Hiroe, ill. II. Title.
PZ8.3.H74 Gar 2001 [E]—dc21  00-010966

Viking® and Easy-to-Read® are registered trademarks of Penguin Putnam Inc.

Printed in Hong Kong

Reading Level 2.4